TREASURE TRAPPED

SIT, STAY, SLEEP COZY MYSTERIES
BOOK 14

PATTI BENNING

SUMMER PRESCOTT BOOKS PUBLISHING

Copyright 2025 Summer Prescott Books

All Rights Reserved. No part of this publication nor any of the information herein may be quoted from, nor reproduced, in any form, including but not limited to: printing, scanning, photocopying, or any other printed, digital, or audio formats, without prior express written consent of the copyright holder.

**This book is a work of fiction. Any similarities to persons, living or dead, places of business, or situations past or present, is completely unintentional.

CHAPTER ONE

A tall man in a crisp white shirt rapped on the wall with his knuckles. "I might be able to do it. I'll have to drill a hole and get a camera in there before I know for sure."

"That would be great." Sadie Barton glanced through the window at the overflowing parking lot then tore her gaze away and focused on the man again. "I wish we could have bought the wireless unit, but it sounded like the signal wouldn't be strong enough to get through these thick walls."

Dave Brown, the IT installation specialist who Sadie had been waiting on for half a day, began making marks on the cinder block wall and muttering to himself.

"Yeah, well, don't get your hopes up too high. In

old buildings like this, you never know what you're going to find. We could still run into issues, and then we'd have to run the wires up the outside of the wall like we discussed before. Wouldn't look nice, but it would get the job done."

"It would look a lot better if you can manage to run the wires inside the wall," she said. "But if you can't, I understand. Do you need anything else from me right now?"

He glanced over at her, seeming annoyed by her impatience. "Well, I'm going to need access to the second story," he said. "It's my understanding that's a private residence?"

"That's right," Sadie said. "It's an apartment."

"In that case, I'm going to need someone to stay in the building while I'm working. Company policy."

She sighed. It wasn't Dave's fault, not really. Well, he *had* been scheduled to arrive between seven and ten that morning, and it was now just after noon and he had only just gotten there, but she was willing to give him the benefit of the doubt and assume that was out of his control.

The truth was, it was *her* fault for thinking the installation of their new intercom system would go smoothly. She had originally scheduled it for Wednesday, but the company had to reschedule, and today,

Saturday, was their next available appointment. She regretted not waiting until the following week.

"You don't need to go up there yet, right?" she asked, well aware that she was practically begging the IT guy to let her go outside. "I could be back in ten minutes."

He looked from her expression to the window and then back again and sighed.

"Ten minutes. That'll give me time to bring my equipment in and use the facilities before I get started."

She flashed him a quick, slightly embarrassed smile and hurried outside through the lobby door before he could change his mind. It was like stepping into another world.

The thick walls that were making the installation of the intercom system such a pain kept most of the noise and heat outside, with help from their air conditioning unit. All of that changed the instant she opened the door. The suffocating heat and humidity of Georgia in mid-August hit her like a wall, and with it came the noise.

Music was playing over a bluetooth speaker in the grassy lawn next to the motel, where a handful of white event tents had been set up. Guests, both current tenants of the motel and day-guests from the nearby town of Greencreek, were already milling around on the grass. She spotted Bailey Tengu at the booth she had set up for her cookie business, Sunshine Desserts. Norma Underwood was there too, not at a booth for her hardware store, but as a guest. Her chunky beagle, Mulberry, was waddling by her side.

Mulberry was far from the only dog in attendance. The event was open to all pets as long as they were kept under control. She saw some of her dog training and boarding clients with their owners, along with some of Allison's grooming clients. There was even someone walking around with a macaw on his shoulder. She stared as they walked past, in awe of the humongous blue bird.

"Sadie!"

She looked over at the sound of her name and saw her best friend, Penelope Montgomery, waving at her from near the corner of the building. Jasper, Sadie's foxhound, was standing next to her, his tail wagging so hard the white tip of his tail was a blur. Sadie walked over to them and took Jasper's leash from Penny. She stooped to greet the happy foxhound, who acted as if he hadn't seen her in weeks, when in reality it had been less than half an hour, then straightened up and focused on her friend.

"How's everything going?" she asked.

"Great," Penny said, beaming. "Cody's in the back, supervising the obstacle course and handing out prizes. The kids love it, especially the ones who have dogs they can take through it with them. Sam's here somewhere… there he is."

Sadie turned to spot her boyfriend, Sam Walker, approaching from where the tents were set up, his two red coonhounds by his side. She greeted him first, with a kiss to his bristly cheek, then reached down to pat the dogs.

"I'm so glad you're here," she said. "I hope you're having a good time. I'm sorry I'm stuck inside with the IT guy."

Sam squeezed her hand in silent reassurance. He was mute and normally spoke to her with sign language, but that was hard to do with only one hand, since the other was currently occupied by the two big dogs' leashes.

"Did he say how long it would take?" Penny asked.

"He doesn't know yet. He still has to figure out whether it's even possible to run the wires inside of the wall."

Penny sighed. "It'll probably be a couple of hours, then. Does he need anything else from us?"

"He needs someone in the building while he's working, since my apartment is a private residence," Sadie said. "So I guess I'm stuck in there with him. I need to go back in soon."

"It just needs to be *someone*, right?" Penny asked. "Not you, specifically? We can take turns, maybe rotate every half an hour or so; you, me, Cody, Maria. We can switch now if you want, or wait until he figures out how long it will…"

Penny trailed off, her gaze slipping from Sadie's face to look over her shoulder toward the parking lot. Sadie followed her gaze to see a tall, broad-shouldered figure stepping out of an expensive SUV. Penny had already pushed past her and was running toward the parking lot by the time Sadie realized who it was. She followed her friend at a slower jog, Jasper trotting neatly by her side.

The figure swooped Penny into a bear hug, spinning her around. Penny's laugh echoed across the parking lot.

"What are you doing here?" she asked when the man set her down.

He reached out and tried to ruffle her hair, but she dodged it easily. She'd had years of practice.

"Why do you think I'm here?" he asked, grinning. "I couldn't miss a party thrown by my little sister, especially not when it's celebrating the one-year anniversary of her new business."

"I didn't even know you were back in the *country*, Justin," Penny said. She gave her brother's arm a light smack. "You should have told me you were coming. I don't have anything ready. Where are you staying? How long will you be here?"

Justin raised an eyebrow. "Well, I figured I'd stay right here," he said. "I've gotta see exactly what the two of you have been getting into since you moved down here."

He turned towards Sadie and opened his arms. She stepped forward for her own bear hug and was grinning like crazy by the time he released her.

"You'll have to wait until this evening to check in," she said. "We're full up now, but a couple of guests have late checkouts after the event ends."

"Sounds fine to me," Justin said. "And to answer your other question, Penny, I'm here for the week. I'll be working remotely for part of the day, but the rest of the time I want to spend with you. You need to show me all your favorite haunts, and introduce me to all your new friends. I want to know everything you've been up to."

Sadie felt a cold nose press against the back of her leg and turned to see that Sam and the two coonhounds had followed them over. She stepped back next to him and linked her arm with his, still grinning like a madwoman. Hosting their parents had been stressful. Hosting Penny's brother was sure to be nothing but fun.

"And who is this?" Justin asked, turning toward them. "A secret boyfriend, Sadie?"

"He's not a secret," she said, barely keeping from rolling her eyes. "My parents know about him, and I'm sure Penny's told your guys' parents too."

"But no one thought to tell *me* the big news? I'm hurt." He stepped forward and held his hand out to Sam. Sadie took the dog's leashes from him so they could shake. "Jason Montgomery. I'm Penny's brother and I suppose you could call me Sadie's honorary brother. It's a pleasure to meet you… assuming you're treating her well."

His eyes narrowed in a threat that was only half joking. Sam gave his hand a firm shake but kept his mouth shut.

"The strong silent type?" Justin asked. "Or you just don't know what to say?"

"Sam uses sign language," Sadie explained. "It's a bit hard for him to talk when you're still shaking his hand."

He let go of Sam's hand and signed a simple

greeting, surprising Sadie almost as much as it surprised Sam.

It's nice to meet you, Sam signed back. *I hope you have a pleasant stay.* His response seemed rather stilted to Sadie, who narrowed her eyes but didn't say anything.

"I think I caught almost all of that," Justin said. "We work with a few charities who are involved with the Deaf community, so I've been trying to pick up some American Sign Language. I'm nowhere near fluent, but I can manage the niceties." He winked and turned back to Penny. "Are you going to give me a tour of this shindig? Is there food here? I'm starving."

"You two go and have fun," Sadie said. She tried to disguise the envy in her voice. It would have been nice to join the celebration for a bit, but she was hardly going to ask Penny to sit out while her brother was there. She would just have to hope Dave worked fast. "I'll join you when I can."

Penny looked crestfallen. "Shoot, I completely forgot."

"It's fine," Sadie said, tacking on a reassuring smile for good measure. "You and Justin need to catch up anyway."

She waved as the two of them walked away. Penny shot a guilty look over her shoulder, but Sadie made a shooing motion. She really *didn't* mind. This was a special occasion, and she was the one who had messed up scheduling the intercom system today, anyway.

I'll keep you company, Sam offered.

"Are you sure? You worked so hard to help us set this up…"

For you, he signed. *The dogs and I already walked around. They need some water, anyway.*

She looked down at the three hounds whose leashes she was holding. Jasper, who Penny had taken for her so she could show Dave the building without being distracted, was only panting a little. The fact that his coat was partly white, and he had been standing with Penny in the shade helped. The two coonhounds, whose coats glowed molten bronze in the sunlight, looked parched. She knew many of the vendors had set water bowls out for the dogs near their booths, but that water was bound to be warm to the touch by now. They had a couple of kiddie pools and dog bowls behind the motel where the obstacle course was too, but it seemed Sam hadn't made it that far before he spotted her.

"Fresh water coming right up," she promised them.

She handed the leashes back to Sam and led the

way into the lobby. Dave was leaning against the wall by the window, looking irritated.

"Can we get started now?" he asked.

"Sorry," she said, realizing it had been a bit more than ten minutes. "Let me unlock the apartment door, and I'll show you where I want the unit upstairs."

She led the way up the narrow stairs to her apartment, kicked her bedroom door shut, then pointed to the patch of wall near the entranceway. Jasper watched the motion, then looked up at her in puzzlement, probably wondering why she was pointing at a bare wall.

"There or close by," she said. "I want it to be central enough that I can hear it from my bedroom if somebody buzzes in the middle of the night."

Sit, Stay, Sleep Motel and Boarding was a roadside motel that doubled as a dog boarding and training facility. The former aspect of their business meant that guests sometimes arrived in the dead of night, long after their employees were gone and Sadie and Penny were both asleep. Their solution right now was to tape their cell phone numbers to the door in case someone needed to check in while the lobby was closed, but that meant anyone and everyone who came to the motel had access to their personal numbers. She suspected some prospective guests might also have been turned away at the idea of having to call someone's cell phone and wake them up in the middle of the night just to get a room.

The intercom system would hopefully help streamline the process for all of them. They were only getting three speakers installed for the time being; one outside, near the lobby door, one inside the lobby since they often used the room for business and personal get-togethers after hours and didn't always want to open the door to a stranger in the middle of the night without talking to them first, and the third in Sadie's apartment.

The system was expandable, which meant they would be able to add more in the future, and it also came with an app so she could get notifications on her phone and speak through the intercom remotely if she wasn't at the motel.

She left Dave to figure out the best route to run the wires and returned to the lobby to refill the water dish for the coonhounds and check the boarding dogs. By the time she returned with Jasper still following loyally at her side, Dave was back downstairs, drawing a final guide on one of the cinder blocks.

"I'm going to drill here," he told her. "I have a borescope camera I'll use to see what the situation looks like from the inside. If it's not going to work out, I'll fill the hole, but you're responsible for repainting it to match the rest of the wall. If you understand the process and agree, I'll need you to sign here…"

Sadie signed the line he indicated on the tablet, then stepped back against the far wall with Sam, watching with mild curiosity as Dave took a drill with a hefty looking bit out of his tool bag and began the noisy process of drilling through cinder block.

He stopped almost as soon as he started and pulled his drill bit back to peer at it. "Huh."

"What happened?" Sadie asked, suddenly worried. Did they have termites? Could termites even live inside a cinder block wall?

"It looks like someone already sealed a hole with plaster," he said. "Come see."

She handed Jasper's leash off to Sam and walked across the room to peer at the crumbling hole Dave was pointing at. He tapped the space around it, and a fist-sized chunk of plaster broke off and crumbled to the floor, leaving a dark hole in the cinder block.

They both stared at it.

"Never seen this before," Dave muttered. "Shoot. I hope it's covered in that release you signed. My boss isn't going to be happy."

"I think there's something inside," Sadie said. She

fished her phone out of her back pocket and turned the light on to look inside the hole, revealing decades-old dust, mouse droppings, dead insects... and a dark brown glass bottle, the top of it tucked up into the hole of the block above the one Dave had broken into.

Sadie would have thought it was nothing but garbage, an old beer bottle someone shoved in the wall as garbage while they were building it, if not for the piece of yellowed paper taped to the bottle that had four words written on it in faded pencil.

To my heart's treasure.

She reached inside and wiggled the bottle around until she managed to get it out without breaking the top off. It had been plugged with some sort of wax seal, which was still intact. There was no liquid inside, but when Sadie held it up to the window, she could see a rolled up piece of paper inside.

She jumped a little when Sam looked at it over her shoulder; she hadn't heard him or the dogs approach. He seemed curious, and Dave looked intrigued too.

"Well?" he said. "Are you going to open it?"

CHAPTER TWO

The lobby door burst open, letting in a gust of humidity, heat, and sound in with it. Penny came in with a bright grin on her face, her brother trailing just a second behind.

"Hey, Sadie, I just talked to Maria and she said she wouldn't mind…" She broke off, looking at the bottle in Sadie's hand. She was still holding it up, and all three of them were staring at it like it was some sort of holy grail. "What is that?"

"We found it in the wall," Sadie said. She turned the bottle around so Penny and Justin could read the note on the side.

"Whoa, that's sweet," Justin said. "It's a secret note. Literally a message in a bottle, except someone hid it in the wall instead of throwing it into the water."

Sam dropped the dogs' leashes, then stepped on them with one bulky work boot to keep them from going anywhere while he signed, *I think we should open it.*

"I have no idea what he said, and I know it's none of my business, but I'm dying to see what's inside," Dave said. "Usually when something 'interesting' happens on a job, it means I drilled into an electrical line or a wasp's nest. I'm dying for a good story to tell that doesn't end with me getting stung or zapped."

Sadie glanced at Penny, who was bouncing on the balls of her feet. "Open it!" her friend said. "What are you waiting for?"

"It could be historically significant," Sadie said, pulling the bottle protectively out of reach. She recognized the glint in Justin's eyes and knew he was about two seconds from swiping it from her. "Breaking the seal might lower its value."

She was mostly just teasing them, but it *did* seem like whatever was inside might be important; something better to open in private. But everyone, even Sam, was watching the bottle like it held the secrets of the universe. There wasn't any *real* possibility of not opening the thing, so Sadie ripped the band aid off or rather, broke the wax seal off the top.

What followed was rather anticlimactic. The paper had been rolled up to fit through the neck of the bottle, but it had unfurled slightly once inside, so getting it out wasn't as simple as tipping the bottle upside down and letting it fall out. Penny ended up running back to her room to get a pair of tweezers, and she and Sadie worked together to tease the paper out without ripping it.

The curled-up paper was clearly old, though less damaged by time than the note on the outside of the bottle was. The wax seal had protected it from the elements, and more importantly, from whatever pests had found their way into the walls over the decades. Sadie set the bottle down on the front desk next to the wax seal and carefully unfurled the paper. Sam, Penny, Justin, and Dave crowded around her to read it, jostling her in their efforts not to be left out. Sadie barely noticed. Her eyes were already glued to the page.

"It's a treasure map," Penny breathed next to her. Justin reached for it, but she smacked her brother's hand away. "It's *our* treasure map. Hands off."

Dave let out a low whistle. "Now, *this* is a story. Mind if I take a picture?"

Sadie was halfway through nodding when Penny gently took the map from her hands and rolled it back up, shaking her head. "No pictures. Are you kidding me? I don't want someone else stealing *our* treasure."

"I doubt there's *actually* treasure," Sadie said. "This has to have been in there for decades. Some kid probably left it as a joke. If they *did* bury something, I'd bet it's long gone."

Penny and Justin looked at her with identical disappointed expressions. Sam patted her shoulder gently, then signed, *It's a treasure map. We have to follow it.*

"This is hands down the coolest thing I've ever found on a job," Dave chimed in. "I'm supposed to be at another job by three, though, and I'm going to need to drill into another cinder block. This one's too compromised to install the unit into."

"What about the hole?" Sadie asked. It looked… bad. Really bad.

Dave gave it a doubtful look. "I'll see if I have the equipment to patch it in my van. If I don't, you'll be on your own. I heard the hardware store in this town is pretty decent. They might have what you need to do it yourselves."

He took one last look into the hole in the wall,

then walked outside, whistling, presumably to check for patching materials. As soon as the door shut behind him, Penny hissed, "Forget about the hole, Sadie. I know you're being a negative Nelly, but just think about it for a second. What if there really *is* treasure? We could be rich! We could afford to have the wall patched with diamonds if we wanted to. And even if there isn't anything there, or it's just some kid's old toy cache, looking for it can't hurt."

It'll be fun, Sam added.

"We could split into teams," Justin suggested. "Whoever finds it gets the biggest cut, but we agree to split the rest between the four of us."

Penny gave her brother a sharp look. "No, most of it should go straight back into the motel. But we could agree to a twenty-percent split for whichever team finds it."

Sadie was about to mention that she was pretty sure any buried treasure or historical artifacts belonged to the state no matter who found it, but she couldn't bear to crush the excitement on their faces. She suspected they were getting ahead of themselves, but Penny was right; she *was* being a negative Nelly. It had been a long, hot, stressful day and she just wanted Dave to finish installing the intercom system so she could go and enjoy the party. Hunting for non-existent treasure was something someone with more free time could enjoy.

But Sam had an excited glint in his eyes, and Penny and Justin shared identical, hungry looks on their faces. She didn't think they would find anything, but if they did… The thought of digging up a buried treasure chest sent a thrill through her. As long as she kept her expectations realistic, it couldn't hurt to have a little fun, could it?

"I like Penny's idea," she said at last, giving her friend a quick smile. "We found the map in the motel, so I think it technically belongs to us or the business. It's fair that most of what we find, *if* we find anything, gets invested into the motel. A twenty-eighty percent split, after whatever taxes or fees we have to pay, seems fair to me."

"If we *do* find something valuable, I'll get my lawyer to look into the laws surrounding this sort of find before anyone does anything with it," Justin said.

"Great," Penny said brightly. "So, the teams are Sadie and Sam, and me and Justin?"

Sam nodded and signed to Sadie, *We'll have an advantage. I've lived her my whole life. I'm sure I can find wherever the map is trying to lead us.*

That was true; they had a leg up on Penny and Justin already. Sadie grinned, finally getting into the spirit of the treasure hunt. "Let's start tomorrow," she suggested. "I bet Cody wouldn't mind some extra hours, and Sundays usually have a lot of check-outs and dog pickups, but not much more going on. He can handle it while we go look for the treasure." She narrowed her eyes. "No one gets a head start. It's not fair if you two get to go out and look for it while I'm stuck here."

"I agree," Penny said. "And I don't think we should tell anyone el…"

She broke off when the lobby door opened and turned around to face it, quickly hiding the rolled up paper behind her back. Sadie expected to see Dave returning from his van, hopefully with the supplies necessary to patch the hole in their wall, but saw Hunter, the young man who made deliveries for Sunshine Desserts, instead. He was accompanied by a young man about his own age, probably one of his friends judging by the way they were talking excitedly together.

Hunter broke off from the conversation as soon as he spotted them. "Hey, Sadie," he said. "Hey, Penny. Eric and I heard something about a treasure map?"

Penny clutched the map more tightly behind her back. "Where'd you hear *that* from?"

"That tech installation guy," Hunter said. "He just told *everyone* about it."

CHAPTER THREE

Sadie saw them coming through the lobby window. Almost everyone and their dog was migrating from the event area through the parking lot to the lobby. Penny muttered an oath under her breath and hurried around to the other side of the front desk, where she quickly locked the treasure map in the drawer under the cash register. She turned the key just in time, because a moment later, the lobby door opened and this time, it wasn't just two people who came in. It was a clump of them, so many people that for a moment they struggled not to get stuck in the doorway.

"Shoot," Sadie muttered. She turned to Sam. "Can you do me a favor and run the dogs back to the kennel real quick? This is going to get chaotic."

He had already stooped to pick up the dogs' leashed and gave a quick nod, hurrying the three hounds out of sight before the room got too crowded.

"Did you really find a treasure map?" someone called out.

"Is this part of the party?" someone else asked. "Are you hosting a treasure hunt?"

"No," Penny said. "No treasure. Go back outside."

"I just saw you hide something in the desk." That last was from Eric, Hunter's friend. Penny gave him a sour look, but it was too late. For the first time in her life, Sadie understood just how real gold fever was. The promise of treasure had hooked the crowd completely.

"Can I get a copy? I'll give you half the treasure if I find it."

Sadie recognized the woman who asked the question; Ginny Kingsley, who owned Loki, a hound mix who had recently passed her Level One Obedience class with flying colors. Unfortunately, her suggestion was popular with the others, who began offering similar deals. Someone even offered to buy the map outright for a few hundred dollars.

When Sam returned from the kennels, Sadie turned to him and, in an effort to keep her question private, signed rather than said, *Why is everyone so excited? Is there some sort of local legend about buried treasure around here?*

Not exactly, Sam signed back. *Six or seven years ago, someone found a tin with some old cash and treasury bonds buried on their property. I think the guy's grandfather buried it there, and told him about it before he died, but word spread and the story grew. People were digging up their yards for a while, hoping to find something similar. The map will remind them of all of that.*

"I'm *not* selling the map," Penny snapped.

"So you *do* have a map?" Ginny said. "You know, you're probably a lot more likely to find the treasure with more people helping."

Penny shot Sadie a panicked look when other people began to chime in in agreement. Somehow, Sadie didn't think the excited group would listen if they were politely asked to leave. Even if they did, there was no way this would be the last time someone asked them for a copy of the treasure map. Darn Dave, Sadie thought. She noticed he hadn't come back from his trip to the van; he must have realized he messed up by spreading the news. That, or he simply couldn't squeeze past the crowd of people at the door.

"Hey, what's all this commotion? I'm gonna need y'all to pipe down."

The crowd shifted as a tall figure in sheriff's garb pushed through from the doorway. Sheriff Islington looked annoyed at all of the people who were still trying to talk over him, but a single glare was enough to quiet most of them. The goatee helped; it made him look like a villain in a western movie.

"Oh, thank goodness," Penny breathed.

"What's goin' on?" the sheriff asked when he reached the front of the crowd. "I half expected to see someone bleeding out on the floor when I got here, what with all the carrying-on."

"They found a treasure map hidden in their wall!" Eric said. This time, Hunter nudged him, looking annoyed.

"You shoulda kept your mouth shut," he muttered. "They might have shared it if we were the only ones who asked about it."

"A treasure map, huh?" Sheriff Islington looked skeptical, but Penny gave a reluctant nod.

"We don't *know* it's a treasure map, but we did find… something… hidden in our wall."

Even the sheriff looked intrigued now, but he turned around and faced the crowd. "The way I see it, it doesn't matter one way or another to the rest of you whether that map is real enough. These two ladies bought this building free and clear, and that means anything they find in it is theirs to keep and do with as they please. I'm sure they don't want any trouble, now. Why don't y'all go enjoy the entertainment they worked hard to set up for you?"

"Hold on," someone said near the back of the crowd. Sadie recognized the lanky, balding man; Calvin Deering, a newcomer to town who seemed to mostly keep to himself. Bailey was next to him, her expression embarrassed but also curious. "The map might have been found on their property, but whatever it leads to probably isn't. It could be on someone else's private property, or on state or federally owned land. I'm sure the county historical association would have interest in it. Did you know there's a museum in Burns…"

Justin, who had been watching the event unfold with an eagerness Sadie knew meant trouble, cut him off. "We've already decided to contact legal experts before doing anything with whatever we find. And of course, we won't enter private property without permission." He paused, then, almost casually, added, "You know, a big, group treasure hunt *would* be fun."

"Not just fun," Ginny returned immediately. "A lot of us could really use the money. I know Ben and I could use it for Stanford Auto, that chain auto shop in Burns has been eating away at his business for months. The money should go toward supporting small, local businesses."

"No way," someone else said. "If I find that treasure, I'm keeping it!"

If looks could kill, he would have dropped dead on the spot from the glare his sister gave him. "Justin, *shut up*," she hissed.

It might not be a bad idea, Sam signed. He was watching the crowd carefully. They had calmed down somewhat with the sheriff's presence, but there was still an eager, hungry edge to them that Sadie didn't like. *You'll be inundated with people trying to buy, or maybe even steal, the map otherwise. If you host an organized treasure hunt, you can control it and make sure the motel gets its slice.*

He made good points, especially since Sadie didn't think there was any actual, substantial treasure to be found. Would she rather deal with people trying to get ahold of the map for weeks or even months to come, or give in, hand out copies of it, and let the locals do all the hard work while knowing the motel would still get its portion if there *was* something to find?

The answer seemed obvious to her.

"Emergency meeting," she said, turning to Penny and Justin. Ushering Sam over, she joined them behind the front desk and they huddled with their back to the crowd. "Sam thinks an organized, public treasure hunt might not be a bad idea, and I agree with him."

Penny gave her a look of betrayal. "We shouldn't have to share our treasure with the town just because *Dave* couldn't keep his mouth shut."

"We won't share all of it," Sadie said. "We could still split it, like we agreed on. We could do a sixty-forty split, with twenty percent going to whoever finds the treasure, twenty percent to be split between the four of us, and the rest going to the motel. Maybe we can set aside a little for charity, too. And that's *if* there's something to find, which there probably isn't."

"The more people looking, the better," Justin said. "I'm only down here for a week, and I don't know about you, but to me, that map didn't look all that easy to follow. I'd love to be the one to find the treasure, but I'd rather *someone* find it than no one."

He has a point, Sam chimed in. *Better for the motel to get sixty-percent of the treasure, than no treasure because we couldn't find it by ourselves. Plus… good publicity for the motel.*

Sadie had to translate for Penny; while she had begun to pick up on more and more sign language in the past year, still wasn't great at understanding it in high-stress situations, when Sam's hands and facial expressions moved faster than she could. In the end, Sadie suspected it was Sam's last point that convinced her friend. A public treasure hunt with a real treasure map that had been found *inside of Sit, Stay, Sleep* would be *great* publicity, especially if they actually found something at the end of it all.

"Fine," her friend relented after a moment. "But we have to do it the right way. Print out copies, make people sign up before they get one… and have everyone who participates sign a contract stating that they only get to keep a *portion* of whatever they find, and only if it's all legal, and all of that stuff. I don't want to land ourselves in hot water by promising something we can't deliver."

"Yes." Justin pumped his fist. "This is going to be fun. I'll get a contract drawn up, don't worry about that. You two handle making copies of the map and coming up with rules. No trespassing, no property damages, that sort of thing. Should we start tomorrow, like we originally planned?"

"I suppose," Penny said. "Most people are free on Sundays, and it's a slow day here, anyway. We're really doing this?" At their nods, she set her shoulders and turned around to face the waiting crowd.

"All right, you win. Everyone who wants to

participate will have to register, and there *will* be rules, but it sounds like the motel is going to be hosting a treasure hunt. Anyone who's interested, we'll unlock our doors starting at nine."

The announcement was met with a cheer. Everyone except for Sheriff Islington, who gave a long-suffering sigh, was happy to be included. Penny looked begrudgingly happy, especially when a few kids began to talk excitedly about how they were going to find hidden pirate treasure, never mind the fact that they weren't anywhere near the ocean.

They managed to get the motel's anniversary celebration back on track without much of a hitch. When Sadie went outside, Dave's van was nowhere to be seen. He must have fled when he saw the commotion he caused, or his boss had decided the whole thing was too much liability and he didn't want the company involved in any way.

It meant she would have to reschedule the intercom installation appointment for a second time, but she didn't actually mind that much; she now had time to enjoy the celebration with everyone else. They locked the lobby behind them as they left, then wandered around as a group, enjoying the fruits of their labor. Penny led the way to the Sunshine Desserts booth, where she talked up the cookies until

Justin agreed to try one, and Sadie stopped to pet Mulberry and tell Norma what had happened when the pair passed them. The older woman hadn't joined the group at the motel, so she was out of the loop.

"Well, that sounds like grand fun for you young folks," she said. She winked. "I don't think these old bones could handle that much hiking around, but that doesn't mean I won't be taking full advantage and running a shovel sale starting first thing in the morning."

Sadie laughed. "I hope you get lots of sales."

She and Sam moved on to the next booth, where she saw another familiar face; Brandon Avery, the man who now owned the Williams' farm; the couple who had owned Angus, the border collie Sadie was fostering, before they died. Except, it looked like he had renamed the farm, because the sign in front of his booth read *Avery Farms Creamery* in big, blocky letters above a cartoon drawing of a cow licking an ice cream cone.

"Hey, Brandon." Sadie waved as she approached. He gave her a polite nod, and tipped his hat to her; it, too, had his new logo on it. "How has everything been going?"

"I'm slowly getting everything up and running," he said. "We're focusing on dairy. It's not usually profitable unless you do it at scale, but I have a cousin in the ice cream business, and he's going to help me get the equipment I need to make and sell my own ice cream. It's probably not what old Williams envisioned when he told me he wanted me to take his farm, but after crunching the numbers, I think it's the best way to keep the farm solvent."

"Hey, it's ice cream," Sadie said. "Everyone loves ice cream, especially when it's about a thousand degrees outside for most of the year. People are going to eat this right up."

He nodded. "That's the hope. Marketing will be important, but I think the farm's made for this sort of small, quality over quantity business venture. I have some samples right here; this batch is made with a traditional style ice cream machine, the kind your grandparents might have had when you were a kid. Right now, all I've got is vanilla. It's more a proof of concept than anything else. Would you like to try some?"

They nodded, and Brandon opened the cooler and passed two small plastic cups to Sadie and Sam. The cups were filled with smooth, creamy ice cream that had little flecks of real vanilla in it. As soon as he passed her the wooden spoon, she scooped a small bite.

Heaven.

"This is *amazing*," she gushed. "Brandon, this is seriously the best ice cream I've ever had."

Sam put his ice cream down so he could fish his little notebook out of his pocket and write, *I haven't had better. The town's going to love you.*

Brandon looked relieved. "Thank you, both. I'm putting everything I have into this. If it fails, that's game over for me. But I think I have something that could be great."

Sadie let out a huff of laughter. "You should join in on the treasure hunt. I doubt anyone will find anything worth money, but you never know."

Like Norma, he had missed out on the commotion, so she gave him a quick explanation and told him to be at the motel at nine the next morning if he was interested. Then she and Sam moved on to visit the rest of their friends and acquaintances before making their way behind the motel where an obstacle course made out of PVC pipes, pallets, and apparently, quite a lot of mud had been set up for the kids and dogs. The obstacles were simple; low jumps, weave poles, a tunnel, and a small maze, but it looked like everyone was having a lot of fun with it.

She and Sam got their dogs out of the kennel and took their turns running them through the course.

Jasper did great until he reached the maze made out of wooden pallets, when he decided to just jump over the low walls and run to Sadie to shake mud all over her. Sam ran both of his coonhounds through it at once, which was a little like herding cats. Everyone laughed when Briar stopped to roll in a muddle puddle, and Sam was grinning by the end, even though he wouldn't win any awards for time.

It was Angus who was the real superstar, though. Cody took him out of his run toward the end of the evening and walked to the beginning of the agility course with the handsome black and white dog trotting by his side. He unclipped Angus's leash, stepped back, and signaled the dog to go.

Angus took off racing like a bullet, completing each obstacle on his own, even the maze, flawlessly. When he was done, he raced over to Cody and leaped. Cody caught him in his arms, mud and all, and praised him between laughs.

Sadie clapped just as hard as everyone else, though she knew the show wasn't *just* a show of the dog's intelligence. Cody had helped her design and build the course, and he had been out here almost every evening, practicing with Angus. It was an exhibition of their combined skills, and it solidified her decision to let Cody adopt Angus. The two were an amazing team, and the fact that Cody had taken the initiative to train the border collie to do something like this on his own time, for no reason other than fun, told her that he wouldn't let the dog languish in boredom, something that was her worst fear for Angus.

The first anniversary party for the motel's grand opening ended up being even more fun than Sadie had hoped, and when they ended the day, everyone was in good spirits. Better yet, the fun wasn't over yet; tomorrow, the treasure hunt began.

CHAPTER FOUR

Sadie woke up early the next morning to take care of the boarding dogs and finish her kennel chores with time to spare before nine o'clock. She hurried upstairs to change out of her scrubs when she finished, and by the time she returned to the lobby, everyone who was connected to the motel was there. Penny, of course, but also Cody and Maria, neither of whom worked Sundays, Allison, who rarely scheduled grooming appointments on Sundays and never this early, Justin, and Sam, who was the only one who bothered to greet her. The others were all raptly focused on Penny, who was typing on her laptop.

She glanced up and gestured Sadie to join her. "I'm finalizing the rules list," she said. "Justin got someone he knows to draw up a contract that should cover our butts if anything goes wrong and should help keep everything legal and make sure the motel gets its fair share if anything valuable is found. I'm going to scan the map and make copies, and people *only* get a copy if they sign the contract and agree to the rules. And one of the rules will be that they can't make or disperse additional copies of the map. I don't want people selling copies."

"It sounds like you've got all of our bases covered, and then some," Sadie said. "Sorry I didn't help."

Penny shrugged. "Justin handled most of it, to be honest."

He gave Sadie a brief salute from the other side of the front desk. "Happy to be of service. Now, can we get started?"

Penny shot him a sharp look. "*No.* None of us are getting a head start. We told everyone to be here at nine, and that's when the rest of us can begin too. It's not going to look good for the motel if half the town shows up to participate in the treasure hunt, and one of us already found the treasure."

"Fine, fine," Justin said, backing down. "Let's at least start printing everything off. I'll help staple the packets."

Sadie read over Penny's shoulder to see what she

and Justin had come up with. The list of rules and the contract were both a lot more thorough than anything she would have come up with, so she didn't have anything to add.

They finished printing the packets out around twenty minutes to nine, and there was already a small crowd of people in the parking lot, waiting for them to open the lobby. The energy inside was almost as excited as the energy outside was. They had decided to search in teams; Penny and Justin, Sadie and Sam, and Allison and Cody were both going to pair up with friends who would be joining them soon. Maria thought the whole thing was a waste of time and had offered to keep an eye on things at the motel while everyone else was busy treasure hunting. A few extra hours of pay for relaxing in the lobby, snacking on cookies, and drinking coffee while she handed out packets to the latecomers must have seemed like a good deal to her.

At nine on the dot, Sadie unlocked the lobby door and, with Sam helping to barricade the doorway, made the waiting crowd form a neat line instead of rushing in like a mob. The two of them acted as bouncers to keep the lobby from getting overcrowded while Penny and Justin made sure everyone who was participating signed everything that needed to be signed before they were sent on their way with a copy of the map.

Sadie was surprised by the number of familiar faces she saw, though in retrospect, some of them were obvious. Hunter was one of the first in line, with Eric, the friend he had been hanging out with during the celebration yesterday, beside him. The two were all kitted out in hiking gear, with collapsible shovels, a physical map of the area, and even a metal detector to share between them.

Brandon Avery was there too, and he was all business as he signed on the dotted lines and received his packet. Sadie could tell that some of the hopeful treasure hunters were more serious than others; for them, the treasure hunt offered a chance to find what might be life-changing money. Brandon was one of those, though he was in the minority. Most people just seemed to be here for a bit of fun.

Sadie would put Bailey in that category; truth be told, she was surprised to see the other woman, since she was as much of a workaholic as Sadie and Penny were and rarely closed Sunshine Desserts for anything, but the true surprise was the person she had chosen to be on her team. Calvin Deering still looked as serious and stoic as ever, even though he carried an old wooden shovel, enough hiking poles for both of them, and a binder of the sort Sadie had used in school. She squinted at it as he went by, but there was no telling what information the pages inside of it held.

Ginny Kingsley and Ben Stanford arrived just a few minutes after nine, but it was clearly later than they would have liked, because they nearly made a scene when they tried to cut in line. Sadie had to threaten to keep them out of the treasure hunt altogether to convince them to go to the back of the line and wait, just like everyone else had to. Ginny seemed to think that just because she was a dog training client of Sadie's, she would be given special treatment, but *no one* was getting special treatment today, not even the staff.

It was nearly ten by the time the crowd began to die down and the stream of people arriving to sign up and get their map slowed to a trickle. They had already let Cody and Allison go half an hour ago, but now the chaos had calmed enough that Sadie felt she and Penny could leave without feeling bad about Maria having to deal with the mess on her own.

"Call either of us if someone causes trouble," Sadie said as she finished signing her own copy of the contract and the rule sheet. "And if someone's being rude or pushy, don't hesitate to kick them out."

"If anyone causes you real problems, call the

sheriff's department," Penny added. "Sheriff Islington called me this morning to tell me both of his deputies are on shift today so they can stay on top of any issues the treasure hunt causes. He thinks, and I agree, that it's inevitable that there will be at least a few instances of trespassing and property damage."

"I'm sure things will be fine here," Maria said. "Good luck out there, all four of you."

They were all eager to get out there and start looking for the treasure, so they didn't stop to say much of a goodbye when they reached the parking lot, they just went their separate ways; Sadie and Sam in his truck, and Penny and Justin in Justin's shiny new SUV. Sadie narrowed her eyes as they drove away. She hoped the SUV slowed them down. She knew how Justin was about his cars getting scratched, and from the looks of the map, the treasure was hidden pretty far out in the dense forest surrounding the town.

She turned to Sam, who was her secret weapon. She was driving today; his job was to try to puzzle out the map and navigate. It was rudimentarily drawn, but a few of the images on it had to be landmarks; a stream or river with an S-bend, a humongous oak tree, a tall rock formation with a split down the middle.

And an X drawn at the top of a hill next to a pine tree sapling.

"Any ideas of where to begin?"

He lay his copy of the map down on his lap and signed, *I think I know exactly where to look. We might have to check a few hilltops, but I know the river and the rock formation.*

She narrowed her eyes. "You've known where to look practically since you saw the map, haven't you?"

His lips curved upward into a pleased smile. *I've been running around these woods since I could walk. The good news is it's on state land. The bad news is that the rock formation is well known, and not too far off a popular hiking trail. The creek bend might hold them up, though; it's about half a mile off the trail in an area that isn't too easy to get to. And the oak... who knows. It might not be there anymore.*

"Well, we've still got a leg up on most people. Let's go."

It seemed Sam was right about the rock formation being well-known; the pull-off near the trail he wanted to connect to on state land was full, and they had to drive a mile further down the road to claim one of the last spots at the next one. It cost them precious time to walk all the way back to the trailhead. Sadie kept checking her phone; if someone found the treasure, they were supposed to call the motel to report it. Nothing, yet. She still didn't really expect to find anything, but it would be a bummer if the whole thing was over before she even got a chance to look.

She and Sam followed the trail to the rock formation, which was just off the path on the side of a hill. A small group was already gathered around it, seemingly debating which way to go. Sam put the shovel he was carrying down so he could talk to her.

Legend has it that lightning split the rock on a clear day when a bootlegger and the chief of police were about to have a shootout. They took the lightning strike as a sign, and ended the confrontation peacefully instead, he signed. *Or that's what my grandfather told me. Let's get out of sight from this group before we leave the trail, I don't want them following us.*

They continued on, following the gradual curve of the trail until they couldn't see anyone ahead of or behind them. Sam pressed a finger to his lips, then carefully stepped off the path, following a game trail through an otherwise impenetrable wall of kudzu. Sadie followed in his footsteps, careful not to damage the foliage too much. She didn't want to make it obvious where they had gone.

They paused about twenty feet off the trail and looked back to see if anyone was following them. This was one of those times when sign language was handy; they silently discussed their next steps; find the S-bend in the creek and then look for the big oak tree from there, but all the while keeping out of sight of anyone else who might be combing the woods. Sam was taking the treasure hunt seriously, and Sadie was beginning to get more into it too. Even if they didn't find anything, this was *fun*.

She took a turn carrying the shovel, so he could use his hands to talk while they walked. They had a few close calls, when they had to duck behind a tree or crouch behind a wall of the kudzu that was slowly eating the forest alive, but they made it to the creek in just under an hour. Sam had been right; they had to climb a steep hill and then slip and slide down the other side to reach it, but hidden in an overgrown valley was a perfect S-bend in the creek.

Sam crouched near the muddy bank and squinted at something on the ground, then gestured her over. *Someone else had been here today.*

Sadie squatted next to him, using the shovel to help her balance. The humidity made everything feel damp, even breathing, and she was pretty sure she had inhaled a mosquito on the hike in, but all of that seemed inconsequential in comparison to the shoe print in the mud.

"I hope we aren't too late," she murmured. She hadn't gotten a call from the motel yet, but service out here was spotty.

Only one way to find out, he signed. *Let's find that oak tree.*

They split up, though they stayed in earshot of each other. Sadie used the shovel as a walking stick, pushing vines and thorns and plants with burrs out of her way as she walked. According to the map, the oak tree had one low limb that pointed the way to the hill where the treasure was buried, but in the decades since the map was hidden, anything could have happened to it. A lightning strike, fire, even rot or bugs could have killed it off. If they *didn't* find it, they would have to begin checking on top of all of the hills in the area surrounding the creek… which meant a *lot* of struggling up steep inclines, something Sadie wasn't particularly looking forward to.

Sweating, and hot enough that the search was beginning to lose some of its charm, she stopped in the shade of a large tree that was completely overgrown and smothered by kudzu and took a sip of her water. It was lukewarm and she would probably perspire it right back out, but it was better than nothing. A fly buzzed around her head; she swatted at it, then leaned back against the tree, looking up into the boughs. It would have been magnificent once, before the invasive vine started slowly killing it. She wondered just how different these woods had been back whenever the owner of the map was alive. Maybe they had sat under this very tree and…

Her thoughts screeched to a halt. She looked up at the mostly dead branches where a few oak leaves clung. At the long limb, not much further off the ground than her head was, stretching away from the creek like a gesturing arm. At the sheer *size* of the tree, which must have been standing there for decades, if not centuries.

"Sam!" she called out in a whisper-yell. When he appeared between two scraggly bushes, she pointed straight up. "*I found it!*"

Now that they had the right tree, it was a simple matter of following where the limb was pointing which turned out not to be so simple after all, since they were lucky to be able to see twenty feet in front of them through the trees, and walking in a straight line was impossible.

Thankfully, Sam had come prepared with a compass. He took a reading and fiddled with the compass to mark the direction they should head, something Sadie pretended she *definitely* knew compasses could do, and they started walking. After a few minutes of struggling through the undergrowth, they found themselves at the beginning of a gentle uprising at the base of a hill.

Sadie stared upwards, her mouth hanging open. This was *it*, there was no doubt in her mind. The pine that was a sapling in the picture was now a towering sentinel on a hill that was otherwise only sparsely covered in greenery.

Sam looked over at her, grinning. *It's up there. I know it is,* he signed before taking the shovel back from her and leading the way up the hill.

He paused when he reached the top. She thought he was waiting for her, since she was following a few paces behind, trusting him to pick out the best way up, but when she reached him, he didn't move other than to reach out and grab her wrist. A warning.

His eyes were fixed on something ahead of them. Sadie followed his gaze and felt her own body lock up when she saw what had shocked Sam into stillness.

The body of a young man lay sprawled in the dirt under the tall pine tree, next to a discarded shovel and a freshly dug hole.

CHAPTER FIVE

Sam dropped his shovel. It was the sound of it hitting the ground that yanked Sadie out of her shock, and they both moved forward together. She realized two things as she got closer; the young man was definitely dead, and she would put money on the large, dead tree branch that lay discarded on the ground next to him being the murder weapon. And she knew him. He was Hunter's friend, Eric.

She remembered watching them sign up for the treasure hunt just hours ago. What had happened between now and then to lead to Eric's life ending like *this*? Where was Hunter?

And where was whatever had been buried in that hole?

Sam touched her arm. He had his phone in his

hands, but pointed at the top corner of the screen; no service. She checked hers too; they had different providers and sometimes one of them would get service when the other didn't. At first, she thought she was out of luck, but then the little "x" in the corner of her screen briefly flickered to a single bar. Her phone lost service again a second later, but it was enough for her to start pacing back and forth on the hilltop, her phone held high above her head.

As she waited for that little bar of service to return, her thoughts zipped around like Jasper when he got the zoomies, except there was nothing fun about this. It didn't feel real, as if some part of her was still standing at the bottom of that hill, grinning at Sam before they started climbing up.

There. She had a single bar of service, and this time it stayed. She gave Sam a thumbs up, then called a number she had saved in her speed dial; Sheriff Islington.

"Don't tell me y'all actually found something," Sheriff Islington said by way of greeting. "Penny'll never let me hear the end of it."

"We found something," Sadie said, grim. "Not the treasure, though. One of the treasure hunters is dead, and it looks like they've been murdered."

What followed was a confusing conversation

where she tried to tell the sheriff how to find them, mostly translating for Sam, since he knew the area far better than she did. The call dropped twice, and finally she just shared her location with Penny and texted the sheriff to let him know to check with her for a GPS marker.

Now that the authorities had their location, all that was left to do was wait. She and Sam hung back at first, but they both knew it would be at least an hour before anyone arrived and they could only hold their curiosity off for so long. Careful not to disturb anything that could be evidence, they approached the scene to get a closer look.

Sadie's gaze skirted over Eric's body. She didn't want to look at him too closely, didn't want to see that blank expression on his face when she still vividly remembered him laughing at something Hunter said earlier this morning. She saw just enough to note the wound on the back of his head; the dead branch had a matching bloodstain. Whoever killed him had taken him by surprise. She just hoped it had been fast enough that he didn't suffer.

The shovel lay in the dirt as if it had been dropped or thrown, but the metal detector was leaning neatly against the pine tree. The hole was about two feet wide and three or four feet deep; he must have been digging for a while, because the ground wasn't soft up there.

She had no way to know if he had found anything, but he must have been relatively certain that *something* was down there, given the effort he had put in to digging. If he had found something... then whoever killed him had taken it.

Do you think it was Hunter? Sam asked when they finally sat down on a rock a few yards away from the hill's edge.

That was the question that had been on Sadie's mind ever since she recognized Eric. They both knew Hunter; he delivered cookies to the motel two or three times a week and often stayed to chat. He could be a little immature sometimes, but while she might not trust him to keep a secret to save her life, she couldn't imagine him outright murdering a friend in cold blood. She knew him better than that by now, or so she thought.

The facts were hard to ignore, though. He and Eric had signed up to participate in the treasure hunt together. Half the town had witnessed them drive away from the motel together. Now, one of them was dead and the treasure was missing.

Maybe, she signed back. It didn't feel right, somehow, to make too much noise on this silent, somber hill with Eric's body still within view and the solitary pine tree standing watch over them. *My gut doesn't want to believe it, but my gut has been wrong before. If it wasn't him, then where is he?*

He could be hurt, Sam signed, though he looked as if he didn't believe it. *Maybe they attacked him too, and he's out here somewhere, trying to find his way back to the trail for help.*

They looked at each other, the possibility distinctly uncomfortable. This was another instance where Greencreek could really use a dog that could track down missing people, but they hadn't found a handler for Sam's two bloodhounds yet, let alone started training them.

"We should look for him," Sadie said, standing up. "If he's hurt…"

But the sheriff asked us to make sure no one interferes with the scene, Sam signed, cutting her off. *And I don't think we should split up.*

"Splitting up is the only thing that makes sense," she argued. "We can't leave Eric alone here, but we also can't leave Hunter alone *out there*. Not if he's hurt and needs help. You should be the one who looks for him; you know the woods better than I do, and you're better at finding tracks and stuff."

And leave you here alone? What if the killer comes back?

"What if the killer is out *there*, looking for Hunter? I don't like the thought of you alone out there either, but this could be life or death for him, Sam. I'll be fine up here. I have my pepper spray, and I can hear and see all around me."

His hands were still for a long moment. She knew it wasn't his own safety he was worried about, though it was certainly one of *her* concerns, rather, his concern for her. He had a protective streak that surprised her, though to be fair to him, she *had* experienced more than a few near-death situations in the time since they had known each other.

But he was a good person, and he knew Hunter nearly as well as she did, and in the end he agreed to go look for him.

If something happens, scream, he signed as he got up. *I won't go far.*

She watched as he began working his way down the hillside, pausing occasionally to check for signs that Hunter had gone by. Only when he was out of sight did she return to the rock to wait and listen and hope she hadn't made the wrong choice by asking Sam to go and look for someone who might not be a victim at all, but rather, the perpetrator.

CHAPTER SIX

In the end, asking Sam to look for Hunter hadn't been the right *or* the wrong decision. He returned shortly after Sadie began hearing the tell-tale sounds of the sheriff and one of his deputies arriving; radio chatter, loud voices, and enough crackling undergrowth and snapping branches to scare away all of the wildlife in the area.

Sam hadn't found any sign that someone injured was wandering around out there, though he did see some disturbed areas that looked as if someone else had walked through in the direction opposite the way they had come.

The strange, not-quite-real feel of the afternoon receded when Sheriff Islington and Deputy Francis joined them on the top of the hill. They took over quickly; after spending a few minutes examining the scene, the sheriff left Deputy Francis to cordon the area off and begin taking pictures while he spoke to her and Sam. They told him everything they could, which wasn't much; a shoe print down by the creek, some disturbed leaves down the hill, and the fact that Eric had left with Hunter that morning, and they had no idea where Hunter was now.

"Well, I don't think any of us expected it to end like this," he said when they were done. "But I'm not surprised, either. Money can make even good men do stupid things. I've asked Penny to request that everyone who signed up for the treasure hunt return to the motel. The two of you are free to head back. I'll be joining you shortly; I've instructed her not to mention the homicide to anyone, and I'd like you to do the same. I'd like to observe reactions firsthand when I announce it."

"We'll keep it quiet," Sadie promised.

Beside her, Sam nodded, and mimed zipping his mouth with an ironic twist of his lips. The sheriff let out a dry huff that was almost a laugh, then sobered as he turned back around to look at the body.

"Whoever did this must have had a good reason. I wonder what they found?"

The hike back to the trail, and then to Sam's truck,

felt much longer than the hike out to the hill had. The sense of adventure and excitement that had given them energy with every step was gone, and now all that was left was sadness, the dull miasma of suspicion, and regret. Sadie wished Dave had never found the map, or at least that he had never spread the news about it. Why couldn't he have kept his mouth shut? Maybe he didn't realize the reaction it would cause, but it was hard to give him the benefit of the doubt when a man had *died* because they were all but forced to make the treasure hunt public.

It was a relief to get into Sam's truck and lock the doors, but it didn't take long for Sam to drive them back to the motel, and as soon as she saw the overflowing parking lot, that relief vanished. In retrospect, the walk back to the truck had been a break; this wasn't going to be over for hours yet.

The lobby was packed full of people; many faces she recognized, some she didn't, and they all ranged from happy and excited to disappointed. As she and Sam wound their way past a handful of people toward where Penny and Justin were talking in hushed tones behind the front desk, she realized the treasure seekers must think the treasure had been found, and were waiting for the discovery to be announced.

Penny spotted them and waved them over. She

greeted Sadie with a tight hug, then to Sadie's surprise, gave Sam a brief hug as well before pulling back and saying in a whisper, "Elliott told me what happened. I can't believe it. I'm sorry, Sadie. This is all Justin's fault."

"Hey." The objection was half-hearted. Justin's face was pale, and he had a smudge of dirt on his cheek; he and Penny had been in the middle of their own hunt for the treasure when Sadie gave Penny her location.

"None of us could have known what was going to happen," Sadie said. "Hold on. Who's Elliott?"

"Sheriff Islington?" Penny said, looking at her like she should know that already.

"His name's Elliott?"

"Yes? What did you think it was?"

"I don't know," Sadie admitted. "I've never thought about it before."

She gave her a *you're an idiot, but I love you anyway* look, and said, "Yeah, well, we've been talking more lately, and…" She shook her head. "That doesn't matter. Not right now. Did he say when he would get here?"

"Soon, I think," Sadie said. She glanced at the clock on the wall. "I should go check the dogs."

"That was the first thing Cody did when he got

back," Penny said. "In fact, I think he's still back there. I didn't tell him what happened, but I think he could tell it was something bad."

"Oh." She was glad Cody had taken the initiative, but it left her feeling out of sorts, like she wasn't needed. But of course, that was ridiculous. She was one of the motel's owners. It was just that the boarding dogs had been her sole responsibility for so long that it still felt a little strange when Cody cared for them instead. She wasn't quite sure what to do with the extra time, and right now, she could have used the distraction.

She stayed behind the front desk with the others instead, leaning against the wall with Sam while Penny twisted back and forth in the spinning chair anxiously, and Justin occasionally reached out to force the chair to stop its repetitive motion.

While she waited for the sheriff, *Elliott*; she didn't know why, but it was weird to think of him as a person with a first name even though he clearly was one, to arrive, she watched the crowd. Many were faces she recognized from this morning, though some must have signed up after she and Sam left.

Bailey and Calvin were standing near the cookie display case, having a whispered discussion. Sadie narrowed her eyes as she tried to figure them out. She knew Calvin had asked Bailey on a date a few weeks ago, and Bailey had turned him down, but the fact that they had signed up for the treasure hunt together seemed to indicate that they were at least friends, if not more. Justin had a bruise blossoming around his eye; Sadie had no idea where it could have come from, but he was far from the only one who looked roughed up.

Treasure hunting seemed a lot more dangerous than Sadie expected. Almost everyone had mud on their shoes, which was to be expected, but quite a few people had managed to get mud a lot of other places as well. She saw more than one shovel with clay-like dirt packed onto the shovel head in chunks that crumbled to the floor each time it was moved. The lobby was going to need to be swept and mopped after everyone left.

The inane thought was whisked away when Hunter opened the lobby door. Her eyes snapped toward him. She took in every detail as he walked further into the room, half-certain he was about to start yelling for help, but the expression on his face wasn't one of fear or horror. He looked curious, a little tired, and judging by the way he kept glancing at his phone, in a hurry.

There was dirt caked onto his boots, a clump of

burrs clinging to the hem of his shirt, and a few streaks of mud on his forehead, as if he had wiped sweat off his brow while his hands were dirty. He lingered near the door, his back to the wall. After a brief glance around the room, he returned his focus to his phone.

He was the last one to arrive before the sheriff. The noise and excitement died down instantly when Sheriff Islington entered the lobby; somehow, everyone who was gathered picked up on his somber expression better than they had picked up on the mood surrounding Sadie, Penny, Sam, and Justin.

"I'm going to ask for patience from y'all," the sheriff said once every eye was on him. "Sit tight for a moment. Penny, can you tell me if everyone's here?"

Penny sat down in front of her laptop and double-clicked to open the file that held the list of everyone who had signed up for the treasure hunt. While she scanned the names, matching them to faces, or occasionally calling out one she didn't recognize, Sadie looked out across the room again. She saw a lot of the people she knew personally who had said they were going to participate in the treasure hunt, except for Ginny Kingsley and Ben Stanford. She knew for a *fact* they had signed up for a packet that morning, but they were nowhere to be seen for now.

In the end, they weren't the only ones missing; a family of four had given up early when the kids got bored, one woman had texted Sadie to say she was at work and hadn't even gone out to look for the treasure yet after picking up the packet, and a few, including Ginny and Ben, simply hadn't answered their phones or the calls hadn't gone through. Some, Sadie guessed, didn't have phone service wherever they were. Regardless of their reasons for not answering, she knew the sheriff would track them down and make a point of speaking to each one in case they had seen or heard something that might be important.

Once they had a headcount, the sheriff cleared his throat and took his place front and center in front of the lobby door. "I am saddened to announce that a tragedy happened earlier today…"

CHAPTER SEVEN

Sadie watched Hunter carefully as the sheriff announced Eric's death. As soon as his friend's name was uttered, his face paled and he slipped his phone into his pocket. She wanted to think it was shock over learning Eric was dead, but she knew it could just as easily be guilt or fear of getting caught.

Her gaze drifted as the sheriff kept talking, not going into details about the death, but making it clear he believed the motive was tied to the treasure hunt. She noticed he didn't mention the hole they had found next to the body, or say anything about the treasure that may or may not have been found. Privately, she suspected that he might get more help from the public if they thought there might be a pot of gold at the end of the mystery, but she supposed that would come with its own share of downsides. She had already witnessed just how far the promise of riches could reveal humanity's worst. Maybe he was right not to bring it up.

Reactions from the crowd ranged from frightened to angry. If Eric's killer was among them, then he or she was doing a good job of blending in. The sheriff spoke slowly, and she knew he was probably scanning the crowd the same way she was, but with a lot more experience under his belt. When he finished giving his explanation of what was going on, he began speaking to each of the hopeful treasure seekers outside one at a time before letting them go.

It was late afternoon by the time he finished. When the last person left and he finished questioning the motel's staff, he spoke to Sadie and Sam again to ask if there was anything else they had noticed or remembered that might be helpful, then finally, *finally* left them to begin to recover as best they could. Penny stepped outside to see him off, and Sadie turned to Sam, who looked just as tired as she felt.

I should go take care of Rose and Briar, he signed. *They've been alone since this morning. Is it okay if I come back later?*

"Of course," Sadie said. "I need to go spend some

time with Jasper and the boarding dogs, anyway. It's been a boring day for all of them."

I wish it had been a boring day for us too, he signed. He left her with a kiss, and Sadie turned to tell the others she would probably be busy with the dogs for a while, but Penny was still outside with the sheriff. She briefly wondered if her friend was getting her own kiss goodbye, and Allison and Maria had left after the sheriff finished questioning them. Cody was outside somewhere with Angus, probably running him through that obstacle course again, which left only Justin. He was sitting in the rolling chair behind the desk, rolling a capless pen back and forth over the surface.

He stopped when he saw her looking at him. "Sorry. Guess I'm not used to feeling like a third wheel. Or, I guess in this case, it would be fifth wheel." His eyes narrowed. "Does that make me the spare tire?"

She let out a breath that was almost a laugh. "I guess it does. Penny should be back soon. The sheriff has a lot to do today."

"She'd better, because I sure have a lot to ask her about *that*," he said. "My little sister dating a cop? I didn't see that coming, that's for sure."

"They aren't dating," Sadie said with relative

certainty. Penny would have told her if it was anything serious or official. She thought, or hoped, things were moving that way for her and the sheriff, but she knew Penny had experienced a streak of bad luck in relationships, and worried that any prodding would only spook her friend and make her overthink and possibly decide that romance wasn't in the cards for her right now after all.

"Well, there's definitely something between them. I'm not blind."

"Sheriff Islington's a good man. You don't have to worry about her."

"No, I'm glad she's interested in someone who's got some teeth. From what Mom and Dad have said, it sounds like the two of you need some extra protection around here. You know, when they said the place was crawling with murderers and other unsavory folk, I thought they were exaggerating." He gave her a pointed look.

She sighed, her shoulders tensing defensively. "It's not *that* bad," she muttered, but she knew he wouldn't believe her for an instant, not after what happened today.

He made a noncommittal noise. "Look, all I'm saying is if you two want a way out, I'll help. And I'll make sure you don't lose a dime doing it, either. If you're only staying because of the money…"

"We aren't," she cut in. If Justin gave them an out this time last year, she might have taken it, but the motel and Greencreek and all of the people and dogs they had come to know and care about here had grown on her like the kudzu vines that had grown over that old oak tree… though hopefully not as damaging as those vines had been to that tree. "Your parents offered too. We aren't leaving. We aren't giving up."

He rolled his eyes as he leaned back in his chair. "You're just as stubborn as she is. It was worth a try. If you change your minds, the offer stands. I don't want to see *either* of you get hurt."

"Yeah, I know," she grumbled. Justin was only a few years older than they were, but he had a habit of chiding them like they were still annoying tweens, and he was the 'wise' teenager giving them advice.

Unfortunately for him, she already knew he gave *bad* advice.

She left him to fiddle with things on the front desk while she went into the kennel room to spend some much-needed time with the dogs. Many of their furry boarding clients were regulars, and their cheerful greetings helped soothe something in her soul. She spent some time in each of their kennels, with a few extra ear scratches and kisses for Jasper and Rosco, who had been boarding at the motel most weekends for an entire year now. He didn't come to stay quite as often as he used to, since after passing both her Level One and Level Two Obedience classes, he was now well-behaved enough to visit his owner's daughter and granddaughter with her. She was proud of him, and happy for both of them, but she missed having him here every single weekend. He had been a fixture at Sit, Stay, Sleep for a long time.

Cody had already picked up messes in the outdoor runs and dispersed midday medication to a Rottweiler with a heart problem, which meant she didn't have much left to do besides take the dogs on their walks and then feed them dinner. She was on the way out the back door with Rosco when he came in with Angus happy and panting by his side, he said a quick goodbye as he closed the border collie in his kennel and began filling a water dish for him. Sadie wished there was time to talk to him about Angus, but he had to get going and she didn't want that conversation to be marred by the disaster today had been, anyway. Tomorrow. She would make the time tomorrow. It wasn't fair to keep them both in limbo any longer than they needed to be.

She lost herself in walking the dogs for a while. Jasper got his walk last, since she could let him off leash and just let her mind drift while he led the way down the familiar paths. Sam caught up with them partway, Briar and Rose both leashed by his side, and they finished the walk together in companionable silence.

CHAPTER EIGHT

It was after seven by the time they finished their walk and returned to the lobby, which meant their open office hours were over. If the weekend had gone differently, they would have had a shiny new intercom system installed and Sadie might have suggested they go up to her apartment for the added comfort and convenience of having the kitchen right there.

It didn't matter; it would have been crowded anyway with the three hounds, Justin, and Penny joining them. The lobby had been a sort of communal meeting ground ever since they first moved to Greencreek, but it was only Justin's presence that made her look at it with new eyes. The lobby was clean and tidy, but other than that, it was… kind of sad.

"Eugh."

Justin made a noise of disgust when he sat down in one of the uncomfortable plastic chairs across from the front desk. He shifted, trying to get more comfortable, but Sadie already knew it wasn't going to work.

"I feel like I'm at a dentist's office," he complained. "Except, it's a dentist's office from twenty years ago, and they like to torture their patients before they even get into the exam room. Which one of you picked these out? Do you *want* to insult your guests?"

Penny, who had already claimed the much more comfortable spinning chair behind the desk, scowled at her brother. "They were already here when we bought the motel."

"Why are they *still* here?"

"Because we can't afford to go out and buy eight-plus brand new chairs?" Penny replied, more snippy than usual.

Sadie knew the events of the day, heck, the events of the entire *weekend*, were wearing on all of them. Sadie leaned against the wall, Sam's arms a comfortable weight across her shoulders, the three dogs tired enough to all try to lay on Jasper's dog bed in the corner at the same time. She wasn't about to interfere in a sibling argument, though it was probably only a matter of time before one of them dragged her into it anyway.

"Dunno why you even need so many chairs," Justin said. "Unless you're expecting all of your guests to sit in here at once, and I don't know why they'd want to do *that*. Why don't you get rid of all of these ugly, uncomfortable chairs and get a couple of armchairs, a loveseat, a rug, and a coffee table instead? You could make a cozy place to sit that's actually *comfortable*."

Penny opened her mouth to argue, then slowly shut it again, meeting Sadie's eyes. She saw her friend's realization that Justin had come up with a good idea, but knew she didn't want to admit it.

Sam removed his arm from around her shoulders to sign, *I volunteer to help you take these chairs to the dump*. He gave Sadie a pleading look, and she laughed for the first time since they found Eric's body. Penny might be too proud to admit they hadn't thought of that, but she wasn't.

"It's a good idea. Let's keep our eyes peeled for a nice, *used* furniture set. I think we should keep the chairs in storage, though; they might come in handy if we ever do another event like yesterday's celebration."

"Yeah, fine," Penny grumbled. "I guess you've

got a few braincells left in that blocky head of yours, Justin." He clutched his heart in mock hurt, but she ignored him. "Anyway, we need to talk about… everything. What happened to Eric, the treasure hunt, whether anyone else is in danger. I wish you'd never found that map, Sadie."

"Blame Dave," Sadie said, though that wasn't really fair either. He'd had no way of knowing what would happen when he picked up that drill. "As far as whether anyone else is in danger, I don't *think* so. It looked like Eric found the treasure before he was killed, or maybe the person who killed him finished digging it up. Either way, there was a hole dug next to him, and Sam and I are almost certain we were in the right spot."

"So there really *was* something there," Penny said with a frown. "In any other circumstance, I'd be thrilled. Maybe whoever took the treasure will try to sell it and Elliot will catch them that way."

It was still weird to hear Penny call the sheriff by his first name; it took her mind a second to catch up, to link the name to the person. By the time she did, Justin was speaking.

"So, do any of you have any likely suspects in mind?" he asked, glancing from Penny, to Sadie, to

Sam. "You must know the locals pretty well by now. Who was the guy who was on Eric's team, again?"

"That was Hunter," Sadie said. "He delivers cookies to the motel. I can't imagine him as the type to kill someone over money, especially not someone he must have known for years."

"It's hard to say," Penny said. "Money makes people do crazy things. It's easy for me to imagine it, two friends digging up a buried treasure on what was supposed to be a lark, only to realize they had something much more valuable than they expected. One of them finds a weapon, and *whack*. That's it. Eric wouldn't have even seen it coming."

I think Hunter is smarter than that, Sam signed. *He would have known how it would look to everyone else. There are lots of places to make a body disappear out there. Why leave Eric at the scene of the crime, especially when everyone knew they were looking for the treasure together?*

Sadie translated for the others, especially Justin who looked like he was giving himself a headache trying to put his scant knowledge of sign language to use, then said, "That's a good point. He could have moved the body just a few hundred yards in any direction, and the chance of someone finding Eric would have gone way down. That makes me think that whoever killed him believed there wouldn't be anything connecting them to the crime."

"It's got to be one of the other people who signed up for the treasure hunt, or maybe even a team," Penny said, frustrated. "I just wish we knew *who*. At least there shouldn't be any reason for the motel to be a target. If the treasure's gone, then the map's useless."

Except most people don't know the treasure is gone, Sam signed. *The sheriff didn't mention that part. As far as everyone else is concerned, there's still treasure out there, waiting to be found. And if you aren't handing copies out anymore…* He trailed off, looking at Sadie. She knew what he was getting at; if someone had missed out on their chance at getting a copy of the map, then stealing the original might start looking pretty appealing to them, especially if they thought there was a buried treasure just waiting to be found.

Sadie told Justin and Penny what Sam had said. Justin looked thoughtful. "That's a good point. One person was already willing to kill for this treasure. It wouldn't surprise me if someone else was willing to steal for it. Maybe I should take the map. I can keep it safe, locked in my car's glove box or hidden in my luggage. No one would know."

Sam shook his head. *That would make the map safer, not the people. If someone threatens you for it…* He glanced at Sadie, *Then I think you should just give it to them. The map isn't worth your life.*

"I agree," Sadie said. She looked at the others. "If someone shows up and tries to bully us into handing the map over, we give it to them and call the police when they leave. We should tell the others too. It's not worth making a scene over. We can ask the sheriff if he needs us to keep it for any reason; if he doesn't, then maybe later this week, one of us can run it up to that museum in Burns that Calvin mentioned."

Justin snorted. "Calvin's that nerdy guy, right? Young-ish, balding, looks like he would wear a pocket protector if anyone carried pens around anymore."

"Wow," Penny said. "That's harsh."

"He's the one who gave me this," Justin said, pointing at the bruise around his eyes. "I figure I owe him a few insults."

Penny frowned while Sadie looked at his bruise skeptically. "When did that happen?" his sister asked.

"When we split up to look for that darn rock formation," he said. "I ran into him and the cookie lady checking out the same area I was."

"*Calvin* did that?" Sadie asked. "Really?"

Justin smirked. "Yep. Swear on my life."

Sadie couldn't imagine it, but if Calvin *had* hit Justin, she was pretty sure he must have done something to deserve it. "*Why?*"

"It's a manly secret," he replied. "Nothing you and Penny need to worry about."

"I'm not *worried*," Penny chimed in. "I just want to get the story right when I tell it to everyone I know."

Sadie and Sam listened to the siblings squabble for a while until Sam checked the time. It was getting late, and she knew he had to be up at the crack of dawn for one of his lawn contracts. He said goodnight to the others, called Briar and Rose over, then stepped outside. Sadie followed him, and they shared a lingering kiss in the twilight.

Be safe, he signed. *I wish things had gone better today, but still… I had fun looking for buried treasure with you.*

"Me too," she said with a soft smile. "I'll see you tomorrow. Goodnight, Sam."

When she went back in, the argument seemed to have died down. Justin had joined Penny behind the front desk, and they were looking at listings for used furniture online. He looked up as the lobby door swung shut behind her.

"You say goodbye to that man of yours?"

"Yeah," she said. "He has to be up early."

Justin watched her for a moment. "You really care about him? He treats you well?"

"I do. And yes, he does."

"Then I'm happy for you," he said. "He doesn't have to talk for me to be able to tell how much he loves you." He reached over to ruffle Penny's hair; she didn't move fast enough to dodge this time, and let out a screech like an angry cat. "Now we've just gotta find my little sis someone like that, and I'll be able to rest easy knowing my two favorite ladies are well taken care of."

CHAPTER NINE

On Monday morning, Sadie woke up expecting some sort of chaos after the weekend. The treasure hunt alone should have been enough to have people at the lobby door at nine on the dot again, and when she added the murder in, she wouldn't have been surprised to find a crowd with pitchforks, or maybe shovels and torches, but there was nothing. It was an ordinary morning.

She got her kennel chores done by nine, and Cody arrived just as the dogs finished eating. Angus bounced straight up and down in his kennel until Cody opened the door and greeted the dog like a long lost friend.

"Have you spoken to anyone who's interested in

adopting him yet?" he asked, looking at the dog rather than her.

This was the perfect time for something positive, she decided. "I am right now."

He turned around to face her, his eyes wide. "Wait, like someone's coming in *today* to meet him?"

"Cody, relax," she said. "I meant you. I've been watching you work with him for the past couple of months, and I can't imagine anyone better for him to belong to."

His face lit up, but then his expression fell. "I'd love to take him, but my mom still doesn't want a dog in the house. I think she's warming up a little, she doesn't mind if I bring him home on the weekends, but she's never liked having pets in the house. And I want to move out, but I can't afford a place of my own."

Sadie felt a twinge of guilt at that. They still weren't paying him very much, just a dollar over minimum wage, a pay raise they had offered both him and Maria once they started seeing a steady stream of income from Allison's grooming business, but he only worked thirty hours a week and while rental prices were low in Greencreek, they weren't dirt cheap. Nowhere was, not anymore.

"If you're serious about adopting Angus, we can

work something out," she said. "He can stay at the kennel during the week for now, and you can keep bringing him home on weekends. I've been meaning to give you a key anyway, you'd be welcome to pick him up whenever you wanted, just leave a note on his clipboard so I don't have a heart attack if I come down and his kennel's empty."

"Do you think that would be fair to him?" Cody asked, hugging the border collie tightly. "I don't want him to have to essentially live in prison because I was too selfish to let someone else adopt him."

"Prison?" Sadie huffed, looking around the kennel room. It wasn't fancy, but it was clean and well organized. Each dog had a good amount of space, a comfortable bed, and access to their outdoor runs all day long, plus lots of attention since she and Cody were in and out of the kennels all day, not to mention their daily walks. "I don't think my kennels are a *prison*. Besides, you're here most of the day during the week anyway, and you already take him home on weekends. I'm guessing you'd take him out for walks or hikes after work at least a few times a week, which means he would only be spending the nights alone here most of the time. It's not perfect, but it won't be forever, either. I'd like to be able to give you another raise this year, and I'm sure you could find a good roommate who likes dogs if you have to."

"I haven't even thought of getting a roommate," he said. "I could start looking right away. And if Angus could keep coming to work with me, then I wouldn't have to worry about him as much while I'm gone."

"Of course," she said. "You would be welcome to bring him whenever we have the kennel space. If we're full, I would probably ask you to leave him at home, but that doesn't happen too often."

She saw his expression brighten again as he thought it through. "You really mean it?" he asked at last. "I thought you wanted him to go to someone with sheep, where he can be a working dog."

"I want him to have a job and not be bored," she clarified. "I'm assuming you haven't changed your mind about wanting a career in dog training. Angus will make a phenomenal demo dog for you, and I hope to eventually be able to host some sporting events here; probably agility and barn hunt at the minimum, but maybe dock diving and disc too, if we can make the space. I'd like to offer classes for all of those as well, which means I'd expect you to train Angus in at least the basics of the various sports so he can be an example to the clients and you can get some experience in it. I think that if you adopted him, he would lead an exciting and active life with someone who loves him. He might not herd sheep, but he would still have a job."

"Then yes," he said. "I'd love to adopt him."

She grinned. "Great. I'll throw together a contract to make it official later today. And I'll stop at the hardware store during lunch to get you a copy of that key."

Cody was on cloud nine for the rest of the morning until Sadie was ready to leave for lunch. She wasn't sure much work was getting done, but she wasn't going to rain on his parade just yet. She remembered how excited she was when she adopted *her* first dog. She hoped she was making the right choice, but she thought she was. Cody was young, but he was responsible and was passionate about working with dogs, just like her, when she was his age.

She finally dragged him out from the kennels so he could watch the lobby while she met Sam at the diner for lunch. It wasn't one of the days when Maria cleaned the rooms, so Penny was busy doing it herself.

One of the nice things about knowing sign language was that she and Sam could have private conversations in even the busiest of areas. They spent their lunch break talking about Eric's murder over their burgers… primarily about who the most likely suspects were. It was hard to narrow it down, because *so many* people had participated, and it could have been almost any of them. She suspected they could remove the families who had gone out with their children from the list, but that still left a lot of people who might have been involved.

A call interrupted their meal just as Sam was finishing the last few fries, and Sadie checked her phone to see Penny's name on the caller ID. She mouthed her name to Sam and answered it, guessing her friend wanted her to pick up some takeout before she came home.

Her guess was wrong.

"Hey," Penny said when she answered. She sounded rushed. "Did you schedule an appointment for Dave to come back and finish the intercom installation today? I don't see it on the schedule and I don't think you mentioned it to me, but I know how insane this weekend was and figured you might have forgotten."

"No, I didn't," Sadie said, frowning. "Why? Is he there?"

"Yeah. Just showed up and started drilling a hole in the lobby wall about a foot down from where he drilled on Saturday. He didn't say anything but 'hi' to Cody, who came and got me because no one told him about any of this."

"I definitely haven't scheduled anything yet."

"Well, he says it's on his schedule. Should I let him do it?"

"I guess," Sadie said. "I think the estimate we signed was good all month, so there shouldn't be any surprise fees. It'll be nice to have it done."

"He says he's going to need me to let him up to your apartment. Should I?"

"Yeah. You have my spare key, right? Just ask Cody to stay in the lobby and keep an eye on things if you don't have time. Thanks, Penny."

By the time the call ended, Sam had already paid. She explained what was going on as they walked out of the diner, then glanced across the road. "Do you mind if we stop at the hardware store? I need to make a spare master key for Cody. We could stop for cookies afterward."

Sure, he signed. *Lead the way.*

Getting a copy of the key made was easy. She chose a blank with a design of a paw print on the top, and chatted with Norma while Sam petted Mulberry and the key machine measured and began to grind.

"Did you get the boost in shovel sales you were hoping for?" she asked the older woman.

Norma gave her a secretive, devilish grin. "I did, and don't tell anyone, but I bumped the price up before I marked them on sale. My customers still saved a little, but I got to pocket more than I would have otherwise. I heard it's a trick the big chain stores use, and I figure they aren't playing fair; why should I?"

"Shady, but smart," Sadie said. "I'm glad someone benefitted from this mess."

"I heard what happened. I'm terribly sorry."

"It's not your fault," Sadie said. "Maybe it was naive to think no one would get hurt. I saw how the crowd was when they first learned about the treasure map."

"Have you heard any whispers about who killed that young man?" Norma asked.

"No. I don't know anything yet. Have you?"

Norma had lived in Greencreek her entire life, and her family had been here for generations. She was the heart of the town's gossip mill.

"I haven't," the older woman said, sounding disappointed. "A lot of people have been asking and also asking me if I knew whether the treasure has been found. Oh, it makes me wish I was younger. I've been wondering if I ought to get out there anyway, give these old bones of mine one last good spin. If Virginia Kingsley can do it in her cast, I'm sure I could manage to dig at least a few holes."

"Ginny's in a cast?" Sadie thought back to when she saw the other woman at the celebration on Saturday, then again Sunday morning. "She didn't have one when I say her yesterday. When did this happen?"

"Oh, I don't know," Norma said. "She came in to ask if I had any metal detectors in stock, and she was wearing a cast that covered her foot and lower leg, everything but her toes. Had crutches too. I couldn't believe she was thinking of going back out there."

"Did she say what happened?"

"No. I should have asked, but she left as soon as I told her I don't have any metal detectors at the moment. I might order some. I think the town's about to go through a new metal detecting phase."

Sadie paid for her new key, said goodbye to Norma and Mulberry, and left with Sam, deep in thought the entire time.

"She must have gotten hurt while she and Ben were looking for the treasure," she said as they walked toward Sunshine Desserts. "I bet that's why they didn't meet at the motel with everyone else in the afternoon."

You sound suspicious, he signed.

"I *am*. What if she got hurt while they were confronting Eric?"

Sadie, Sam signed, finger spelling her name in a way she knew meant he thought she was missing something obvious. *She was looking for a metal detector this morning. Whoever killed Eric took the treasure with them. If she already had the treasure, why would she want to keep looking for it?*

"Oh. That's a good point."

He patted her shoulder, kissed her cheek, then held the door to Sunshine Desserts open for her. Bailey was placing fresh cookies in one of the displays, but put the tray down and turned to greet them as they came in.

"My two favorite customers," she said with a smile, wiping her hands on her apron. "What can I get for you today?"

They perused the display case. Sam decided to try a cherry amaretto cookie with cherry jam in the center, and after a long deliberation, Sadie chose a s'mores cookie, a seasonal offering that she hadn't had since last summer.

As Bailey rang them up, Sadie asked, "How's Hunter doing?"

The other woman sighed. "He's having a tough

time of it. I told him to take a few days off. I think it's the guilt that's really getting to him, you know?"

"The guilt?"

"Well, he and Eric signed up for the treasure hunt as a team, but he said they decided to split up partway through the morning so they could cover more ground. And that's the last time he heard from him. He had been trying to call and text him for hours, but when Eric didn't answer, he thought he was just somewhere without any service. I think he feels like if they hadn't split up, Eric would still be alive."

That explained a lot. Sadie thought the story seemed not just plausible, but likely, and for the first time allowed herself to feel empathy toward Hunter rather than suspicion.

"That's a horrible weight for him to have to carry," Sadie said. "I hope he's all right."

"Me too," Bailey said. "I told him he doesn't have to worry about his job. He can take the time he needs, visit his family, whatever helps. That means I might be dropping off deliveries for a while."

"Well, you know we're always happy to see you at Sit, Stay, Sleep." Mentioning the motel reminded Sadie of Justin and his bruised eye. "Hey, I've got a weird question and I don't want you to think I'm mad, but… did Calvin punch someone in the face yesterday?"

Shock rippled across Bailey's face. A second later, she burst out laughing. "Sorry," she wheezed. "Who told you *that*? Lord, no. That's not what happened. That Justin guy was following us up this steep hill, practically a cliff, chattering away. I think he thought we knew where we were going and was trying to distract us. Well, we had no idea where we were going, but the distraction worked. A rock slipped out from under my foot and I started to fall, but Calvin managed to catch me. That unbalanced *him,* and he fell backwards, pinwheeling his arms right into Justin. They both tumbled a good twenty feet down the hill. Our best guess is that Calvin's elbow hit him on the way down. He said not to tell anyone, that he would make up a cool story for it. I didn't realize that was what he meant."

Now, that story made more sense to Sadie than Calvin punching Justin out of the blue. Sam was chuckling as they left.

You should definitely tell Penny the truth, he signed to her as they walked toward his truck. *But wait until I'm there. I want to see the look on her brother's face when he realizes we know what really happened.*

CHAPTER TEN

Sadie was just about to say goodbye to Sam when her phone rang again. He looked amused at her exasperated sigh and leaned against his truck, waiting while she checked the caller ID. It was an unknown number, but the area code was local. She answered it with a cautious, "Hello?"

"Hi, Sadie. This is Brandon Avery. I hope I'm calling the right number. I remembered you called me once back when all that nasty business with the Williamses was occurring, and found this number in my call history."

"Yeah, you have the right number," she said. "What can I help you with? If this is about Angus, I've already found him a new home."

Brandon had ended up inheriting the Williams'

property, and there had been a possibility that could have included Angus, but the sheriff had told her weeks ago that no one involved wanted to adopt him, and she was free to re-home him if she wanted to. Still, she was worried something would happen and someone would try to take him away from Cody. The sooner she drew up a contract and had Cody sign it, the better.

"No, it's nothing to do with that," he said. "Honestly, I wasn't sure who to call, but I figured you would know what to do. I'm not certain, but I think I might have found the buried treasure."

Sadie wasn't sure what expression her face made, but she must have looked shell-shocked because Sam pushed away from his truck and signed, *What?*

She held up a finger and quickly said into the phone, "What do you mean, Brandon? Where did you find it?" She hesitated, then added, "What is it?"

"It's not anything valuable," he said. "I don't think so, anyway, but what do I know? Looks like a bunch of old letters written to and from someone from the Underwood family. And I mean *old.* The paper they're written on looks like it should be in a museum. I found them in an old, rusty box in the ditch along the road not far from where that young man's body was found. I figure someone might have tossed the box out of the car, because the thing was busted open and some of the letters had been blown around."

Old letters with the Underwoods name on them. Sadie knew the Underwoods had been in town for generations; the box certainly could be what Eric dug up before he was killed.

"Thanks, Brandon," she said after a second. "You should call the sheriff's department and let them know what you found."

"Well, if they don't want the letters, what do you want me to do with them?" he asked. "I'm sure they're of historical significance to somebody, but it isn't the sort of thing I'm interested in."

"If the police don't need to take the letters into evidence, then I'll come pick them up from you," Sadie said. She was curious to see what was in them, even if she and Penny didn't end up keeping them. Norma probably had a better claim than they did, or maybe the museum in Burns would want them.

"Alrighty," he said. "I'll give the authorities a call once I get off the phone with you."

She thanked him and ended the call, then told Sam what was going on. He looked as intrigued as she felt.

Do you think it's what the map led to? he signed.

"It must be," she said. "It's way too much of a coincidence otherwise, isn't it?"

So, whoever killed Eric found that box, Sam mused. *But when they opened it and saw that it was nothing but a bunch of letters, they got upset and threw it away?*

"They killed Eric for nothing," Sadie said, her stomach twisting. Somehow, that made it worse.

Do you want to check the area where Brandon found the box? he asked. *In case he missed some of those letters.*

"Do you have time?" she asked. "Cody and Penny can take care of things at the motel for a while longer, but I know you have to work, and I don't want to make you late."

My next lawn isn't urgent, he signed. *The property owners are out of town, I don't even have to get it done today, as long as I do it this week.*

"Let's do it, then," she said. "I have to admit, I'm curious to see some of those letters for myself. I have no idea whether we'll be able to have the ones Brandon found or not, so this could be our only chance."

She got into Sam's truck and nibbled on her s'mores cookie while he drove them back toward the spot where they started their search for the treasure the day before. As they neared the turnoff where the trailhead began, she leaned forward in her seat and said, "Wait, I think I recognize that vehicle."

He slowed the truck and came to a stop on the shoulder just inside the muddy turnoff.

"Yeah," she said, "I'm pretty sure that's Ginny's. What's she doing out here? Maybe Norma was wrong about her being in a cast. I can't imagine someone would go hiking with a broken leg."

Someone's in the car, Sam signed. *Look.*

She squinted, trying to peer through the tinted back window. Sure enough, she saw the back of someone's head turn slightly in the driver's seat. Without her having to ask, Sam put the truck into gear and pulled into the parking area, taking a spot a few feet down from Ginny's vehicle.

He waited in his truck, though kept a sharp eye on her as she got out and walked over to Ginny's car. As she approached, the other woman rolled down the driver's side window.

"Hi, Sadie," Ginny said. "Are you here to look for the treasure too?"

"No, Sam and I were just driving past when we saw you," Sadie said. "Norma mentioned you were in a cast when she saw you this morning. Is everything all right?"

She could see crutches lying in the back seat, which told her Norma hadn't been dreaming things up.

"Ugh, I should have known she would tell everyone," Ginny said. "It's a boring story. Ben recognized the rock formation on the map, so we set out to this trail straight away. About ten minutes after we started hiking, I slipped and had a pretty bad fall down a hill. Ben had to carry me out, and he drove me straight to the hospital. I don't know what I would have done without him. As it turns out, I broke my ankle."

"That's horrible," Sadie said. "I'm sorry. It sounds like a lot of people got hurt yesterday."

"Oh, you don't have anything to apologize for. This was my own fault. I was too eager to find the treasure, and forgot to be careful. Mostly, I just feel bad for Ben. He wanted to find the treasure so badly. He's out there now, looking for it. I can't go with him, of course, but I volunteered to wait for him out of solidarity."

"Did he wait with you at the hospital all day?"

"He would have," Ginny said with a secretive, warm smile. "But I told him there was no sense in him waiting. It wasn't as if I was on death's door. I told him he might as well go back to the shop and get some work done, instead of letting the whole day go to waste. At the time, I was hoping I had only twisted it, and I might be able to rejoin the treasure hunt later. Oh well, I'm just glad he's getting a chance to look now. I was hoping he'd have the woods to himself, but it seems we weren't the only ones with this idea."

"What do you mean?"

"I saw that young man who delivers cookies for Sunshine Desserts walk past not long ago, carrying a shovel. He looked like he knew where he was going, too."

Sadie frowned. Hunter was out here, and so was Ben. If neither of them knew the treasure had already been found, they might get into a disagreement trying to be the first one to find it. If one of them *did* know that the treasure was gone, then that meant that person must be the killer. Either way, she didn't see this ending well.

"I think Sam and I might take a walk after all," Sadie said. "I hope you feel better soon. I'm sorry about your ankle."

Ginny said goodbye and rolled her window up, and Sadie returned to Sam's truck. "Ben Stanford and Hunter are both out there, looking for the treasure," she said as soon as she sat down.

You're worried, Sam signed.

"A little. We should at least go and warn them that the treasure was already found."

Neither of them had been planning on a hike today, but thankfully both of them wore sturdy, functional clothing for their jobs so they didn't fare too badly. The first part of the hike was easy enough, since they simply had to follow the path. The going became a little slower once they had to leave the path and hike cross country, but the fact that they both already knew where they were going made things a little easier. They made good time and were able to bypass the creek entirely, sticking to higher and drier ground.

Sweaty and bug-bitten, by the time they neared the hill Sadie began to wonder if they were doing all of this for nothing. But then she heard the voices, *shouting,* coming from the direction of the hill with the lonely pine tree on it.

She and Sam exchanged a look and quickened their pace.

CHAPTER ELEVEN

Sadie wasn't in terrible shape, but she wasn't exactly the most fit person either. She got out and exercised with the dogs every day, but that didn't exactly make her a marathon runner, and jogging uphill was something she usually avoided like the plague. That meant she was huffing and puffing as she and Sam scurried up the hill, trying to be both fast and quiet.

As they got closer, she could make out Hunter's voice better. "Stop! Get away from me."

The shout sounded frightened, and she hurried faster despite the stitch in her side. She had no idea what was going on, but it didn't sound good. She frowned, thinking about Ginny's story. Ginny said Ben drove her to the hospital, but hadn't stayed. What if he had returned to the woods instead of getting some extra work done at his auto shop like Ginny thought? Sadie already knew the treasure was important to him; just yesterday, Ginny mentioned that his business wasn't doing well thanks to the cheaper prices and faster service the nearby chain shop in Burns could offer.

She had met Ben a few times, and just by looking at him she could tell he was a strong and capable man. Plus, he had been having an affair with a married woman, which told Sadie his morals were questionable at best. He had it all; the desperation to be willing to murder someone for riches, the strength to pull it off, and weak enough morals to give in to his greed, even if only for a moment.

She couldn't imagine Hunter murdering his friend in cold blood, but Ben? That didn't seem quite so impossible.

When she finally reached the top of the hill, she saw Hunter standing with his back to the pine tree, swinging his shovel back and forth in front of him defensively. Ben had his own shovel held up like a weapon and was slowly circling Hunter, looking for an opening. Hunter already had a bleeding gash on his temple, as if Ben had gotten one hit in already.

"Just leave me alone," Hunter said, his voice

cracking. "Someone already dug up the treasure. Can't you see the hole?"

"There has to be more there," Ben said. "There has to be."

He sounded half crazed and half like he was trying to convince himself. Sadie could imagine his rage when he finally got that box back to his vehicle and looked inside, only to discover that it wasn't what he had hoped. Maybe he really did believe there was something else buried deeper, or maybe he was just hoping he hadn't killed Eric over a bunch of letters that were worth nothing to him.

Either way, he had Hunter in his sights now. Sam had stooped to grab a big stick from the ground, but he couldn't shout, which left it to her to draw attention to the two of them.

"Hey!" she called out.

Ben whirled on them, surprised and furious to see the two of them. "What are you doing here?" he snapped. "The treasure is mine!"

"The treasure was a box full of letters," Sadie said. "That's all it was. You know that."

He shook his head. "No. There has to be more here than that rusted tub of love letters. There *has* to be. I need this. Just one lucky break. That's all I need."

"What is he talking about?" Hunter called out. He looked relieved to see them, though his back was still pressed to the tree and it didn't look like he was going to let go of his shovel any time soon.

"Someone found a rusty box full of decades-old letters in a ditch not far from here," Sadie explained. "I think they're what Eric found before he was killed."

"There has to be more buried further down. I just haven't found it yet," Ben insisted.

"I think he killed Eric," Sadie said, seeing that the younger man was still confused. "Eric found the treasure, but then Ben found him."

"It was supposed to be gold," Ben continued, babbling. "I didn't know it was letters. Useless," he muttered. "I wouldn't have done it if I'd known."

Slowly, Hunter's fear turned to shock, and then anger. "Dude. Eric had just gotten accepted to an out-of-state college after *years* of taking classes online. He had a girlfriend and a cat, and he loved bowling. I've known him since kindergarten, and you killed him over a box of useless old letters?"

"There's more buried here. I can feel it," Ben said. He turned, and Sam tensed, but he didn't make a move toward Hunter. Instead, he returned to the hole and began digging as if his life depended on it, muttering under his breath as he tossed shovelfuls of dirt to the side.

Giving Ben a wide berth, Hunter inched around the outskirts of the hill to join Sadie and Sam.

"What now?" he whispered. "This guy has gone completely insane."

"Now we call the sheriff's department," Sadie said. "And work, too. I think I'm going to be getting back to the motel a lot later than I meant to."

EPILOGUE

"Where have you been?" Penny asked as Sadie stepped into the lobby two hours later. "Cody said you'd been held up, but I couldn't get a hold of you. I was getting worried. You'll never *guess* what happened while you were gone."

Sadie, who was covered in bug bites and had a dehydration headache, stopped in her tracks and glanced over at her friend.

"What?"

"Cody caught Dave, the IT guy, trying to break into the cash register. He took a video of it, smart boy, then came to get me. I confronted Dave and he said he was looking for the map. *Apparently* he just wanted a copy of it since he missed out on his chance to get one yesterday." Penny scoffed. "I told him he was out of luck and sent him packing, and I called his boss too, for good measure. I know we said we'd hand the map over if someone tried to steal it, but there was no way I was letting that guy walk away with it. So yeah, I'm pretty sure he's going to get fired and we might even get the installation for free. I think he finished installing the intercoms before I kicked him out, too. Cody and I tested the one between the outside and the lobby, and it worked great. You'll have to test the one in your apartment." She paused, took a deep breath, then said, "What happened to you?"

"Not much," Sadie said casually. She grabbed a water bottle off of the display where they kept the cookies. "Just caught Eric's killer, saved Hunter's life, and figured out what the treasure was."

Penny stared at her. Sadie took a long swig of the water, drawing it out on purpose, knowing it would drive her friend crazy.

"Oh my gosh," Penny finally said. "Stop drinking! What are you talking about? What happened? Who killed Eric?"

"It was Ben Stanford," Sadie said. "Yesterday, Ginny mentioned his business wasn't doing so great. He thought the treasure would give him the chance he needed for a fresh start. Except, it turns out the treasure was a box full of old love letters that Brandon Avery found tossed in a ditch on the side of the road not far from the spot where Eric was killed. Ben was furious when he realized the treasure wasn't going to make him rich, and he went back to the same spot today to try to dig the hole deeper and see if he had missed something. Hunter had the bad luck to show up at the same time. Thankfully, Sam and I intervened before anyone got hurt, but it was a close call."

"Okay, your story is way more interesting than mine," Penny said. "Is everyone okay? Did they arrest Ben?"

"They did," she said. "He didn't stop digging until they got there. He must have made it another two feet further down, and that was rocky soil, so it can't have been easy. Hunter said it best; it was like Ben completely lost his mind."

"I can't even imagine," Penny said. "Poor Hunter, poor Eric, poor everyone." Her expression darkened. "I wish Dave had never found that map. Or at least that he had never spread news around."

"Me too," Sadie said. "I think a lot of people made mistakes, though, not just him."

"Did you get a chance to read any of the letters?"

"I haven't yet," Sadie said. "But the sheriff said he should be able to get them back to us within the next couple of weeks, if everything goes well. I don't know what we'll do with them, but at least it's *something*. Maybe we can donate them to that museum Calvin mentioned, along with the map. Or see if Norma wants them, since it was her family name on the letters."

"Well, we're definitely reading them first," Penny said. "But after that, yeah. I think the public deserves to see them. They should get *some* good out of this mess."

"Is Cody still here?" Sadie asked as she finished her bottle of water.

"No, he left with Angus a while ago. We didn't exactly have much else going on today, so I told him he could leave a little early. Oh, before I forget, someone called and asked if you could help with catching a loose dog."

Sadie, who was on her way back to the kennels to check on the boarding dogs, paused and looked over her shoulder. "Sure, I can give it a try. I still have that live trap I bought last year. Did they give any details? Where are they located?"

"They're out in the country somewhere," Penny said. "I don't think they're too far from here. The woman who called said her mother is convinced the dog is a ghost, and she just wants someone to catch the dog and get it off the property so that her mother stops calling her in a panic every time she sees it."

"I'll call them tomorrow," she said.

A ghost dog and a frightened woman. Sadie already knew she would try to help, but not right this second. She needed a break before she dove headfirst into something new.

Printed in Dunstable, United Kingdom